Patience

BY CYNTHIA AMOROSO

The Child's World

Published by The Child's World®
1980 Lookout Drive • Mankato, MN 56003-1705
800-599-READ • www.childsworld.com

Acknowledgments
The Child's World®: Mary Berendes, Publishing Director
The Design Lab: Design
Pamela J. Mitsakos: Photo Research
Christine Florie: Editing

Photographs ©: David M. Budd Photography: 7, 9, 11, 13, 17; iStockphoto.com/
caracterdesign:15; iStockphoto.com/EricVega: 21; iStockphoto.com/erierika:
cover, 1; iStockphoto.com/FrankyDeMeyer: 19; iStockphoto.com/Ju-Lee: 5.

ISBN 9781623235222
LCCN 2013931451

Printed in the United States of America
Mankato, MN
July, 2013
PA02172

ABOUT THE AUTHOR

Cynthia Amoroso is Director of Curriculum and Instruction for a school district in Minnesota. She enjoys reading, writing, gardening, traveling, and spending time with friends and family.

Table of Contents

What Is Patience?

Waiting for something can be hard! You might need to wait for your school bus. You might have to wait in line at the movies. Patience means staying calm while you wait. It means not getting angry or upset.

Patience means staying calm when waiting for the school bus.

Patience in the Classroom

Sometimes schoolwork can be hard. Maybe you have a question in class. You raise your hand for help. But other students have questions, too. The teacher cannot help everyone at once. You show patience by not waving your arm. You wait calmly until the teacher gets to you.

You can show patience in your classroom by waiting your turn.

Patience at Home

Maybe you had a long day at school. But there is some nice new snow outside. Your dad has said he will take you sledding. You would like to go right away! But your dad says you must wait. He needs to shovel the sidewalk first. You show patience by not getting upset.

Patience can mean waiting quietly while someone finishes a job.

Patience and Games

You are playing a game with your sister. She has never played this game before. You need to **explain** the rules. You must explain them two or three times. You show patience by taking your time. You stay calm while your sister learns how to play.

You can show patience when someone is learning something new.

Patience and Sports

Maybe you like to play ice hockey. You love to skate fast and try to score. You would like to play the whole game! But there are lots of kids on your team. They all like to play, too. You must sit out while they take turns playing. You show patience by not getting angry. Watching them play can be fun!

Patience means waiting while people take turns.

Patience on Vacation

You go on vacation with your family. You are going somewhere far away. It is a long drive. You can hardly wait to get there. You want to go swimming. But you know that getting angry will not get you there faster. You show patience during the drive. You sit quietly and do not get upset.

Sometimes long drives take lots of patience.

Patience and Lines

Lines are everywhere! You wait in line to use the slide. You wait in line at the lunchroom. Waiting in line is no fun. Sometimes kids cut in front of others. But you know that is not very nice. You show patience by waiting your turn.

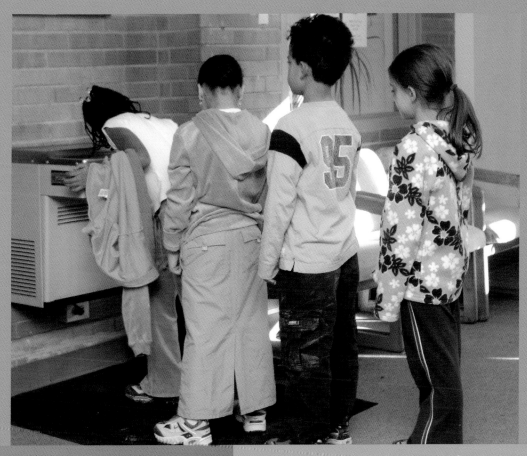

Waiting in lines takes patience!

Patience and You

Learning new things takes patience. Maybe you are learning to play the piano. Maybe you are learning to dance. You make lots of mistakes at first. But you keep **practicing**. You show patience by not getting upset at your mistakes. You keep trying your best. You know you will get better!

It takes patience to learn a new song.

Patience Can Be Hard!

Being patient is not always easy. Sometimes we want things to happen quickly. It is easy to feel upset when they do not. But getting upset makes the wait seem even longer. And getting upset is hard on the people around you. Showing patience is a nicer way to treat other people. It makes you feel much better, too!

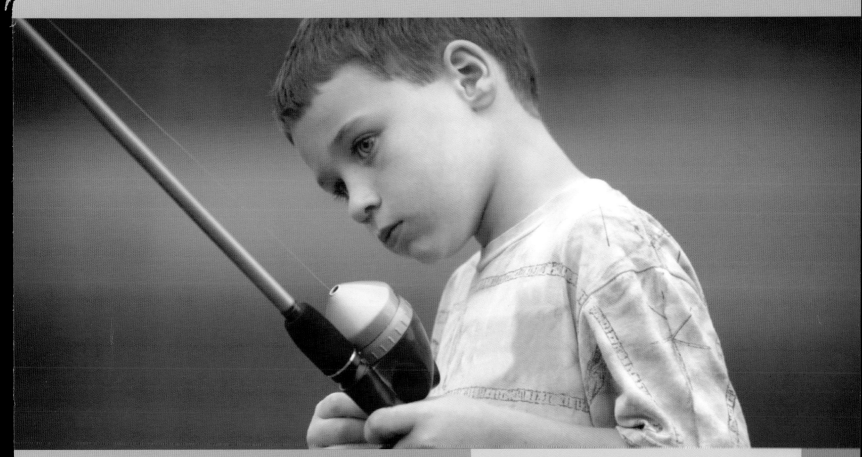

Fishing takes a lot of patience.

Glossary

explain–To explain something is to tell how it works.

practicing–Practicing means doing something lots of times so you get better at it.

Learn More

Books

Berry, Joy. *Let's Talk About Being Patient*. New York: Joy Berry Books, 2010.

McGuire, Andy. *Remy the Rhino Learns Patience*. Eugene, OR: Harvest House Publishers, 2010.

Web Sites

Visit our Web site for links about patience: **childsworld.com/links**

Note to Parents, Teachers, and Librarians: We routinely verify our Web links to make sure they are safe and active sites. So encourage your readers to check them out!

Index